To my nephews,
Andrew and Blake,
I am so proud to be your aunt.
Watching you both grow into the young men you are
today has brought me so much joy.
Always count your blessings and stay close to God.

Love
Aunt Rachel

# Andrew and Blake

## Count Down to a Clean Room

By Rachel Carr

Andrew and Blake wanted to
go to the beach to play.
Their mother said they had to
clean their room first. Can you help them
clean their room so they can go play?

As the cleaning began, they found..

Andrew

Blake

# 20

## Twenty
## Seashells

# Which is the biggest shell?

# 19

## Nineteen
## Dirty Clothes

# Can you find the one with a dinosaur on it?

# 18

## Eighteen
## Socks

**Find the pair that match.**

# 17

## Seventeen
## Sports Balls

# Which one is the basketball?

# 16

## Sixteen
## Trucks and Cars

# Find the ones that are the same.

# 15

## Fifteen
## Toys

Which toy is your favorite?

# 14

**Fourteen**
**Pieces of Trash**

**Can you help throw the trash away?**

# 13

**Thirteen
Books**

# What is your favorite book?

# 12

**Twelve
Toy Construction
Vehicles**

# Which two are alike?

# 11

## Eleven
## Things for Fishing

# Which ones do you put in a tackle box?

# 10

**Ten
Different Cups**

**Find the measuring cup.**

# Nine
# Toy Dinosaurs

**What is your favorite dinosaur?**

# 8

## Eight
## Army Men

**Find the ones that are alike.**

# 7

## Seven
## Different Games

**What is your favorite game?**

**Six
Tracks**

**Which track can you not drive a car on?**

# 5

## Five
## Baseball Cards

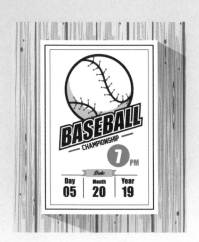

# Do you like baseball?

# 4

## Four
## Dirty Towels

**Place the towels in the laundry basket.**

# 3

## Three
## Flying Toys

**Which one goes into outer space?**

# 2

## Two
## Made Beds
### Did you make your bed today?

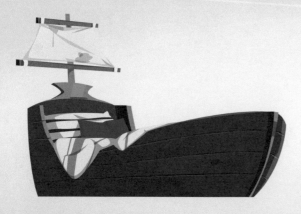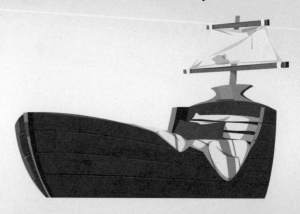

# 1

## One
## Clean Room

Andrew

**Blake**

**All done!**
**Andrew and Blake**
**can now play in the sand.**

# THE END !

# Enjoy our other books with more coming soon !

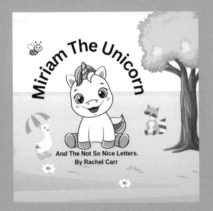

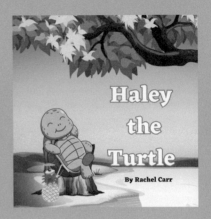

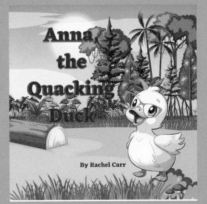

Rachel was born and raised in Tennessee, where she is now raising her 4 children with her loving husband. She enjoys writing books that inspire children to read. Growing up with dyslexia herself brings an understanding of what difficulties some children face. She hopes her books bring others as much enjoyment as writing them has brought to her .

Made in the USA
Columbia, SC
15 October 2024